I0538334

For Jessica and Marleija,

Thank you again for the tea.
Tons and tons of luck to you both.

Roadside Attraction

Part One

Siren Night

***

Keith Blenman

ISBN: 978-0-9890234-2-9

Let’s start from the beginning.

No. On second thought, let's start near the end.
We can always go back later.

A thing about The Boss is, I've seen his pecker more times than I'd care to remember. For the rest of the knowing world, he grants the courtesy of dirty jeans and enormous belt buckles. For me, I get the whole spread on any number of unwarranted occasions. Just today I've endured it three times already.

You see, The Boss only sleeps naked.

This morning I woke up him up in a Florida motel to tell him I had a lead on a hunt. All along the Gulf of Mexico, men had been disappearing from small towns. We arrived in Palm Harbor too late to catch our prey, but on the radio I'd heard a report about a missing father of two on Dauphin Island, somewhere in Alabama. One night he'd been in a karaoke bar. The next day he was gone. Shortly after, his bones were found picked clean in a swamp. It must be a small community, because it only took the forensic odontologist two days to ID him.

On its own the news seemed random, but it wasn't the first time a lousy singer had gone missing and turned up as a pile of scraps. Besides, it was as close to a lead as we had, and the nine hour drive seemed to correlate with our prey. So, what did I do? I nudged The Boss's hairy back to tell him the news. And what did he do? He scratched his beard, tossed the sheet aside and sat up. And there it was, right before me, standing at attention like wounded soldier wanting back in the fight. "We best get goin' then," The Boss told me. "You drive, Millie. I feel like drinkin'."

A thing about The Boss's pecker is, it has scars. Two faded slashes running parallel from the middle-left to the top of the tip. They split the circumcised rim and leave grooves almost to the end. Out of all The Boss's scars, they're among the smallest. Out of all his scars, they're the two that give me chills.

The Boss slept and snored rum breath for most of the drive. It turned out Dauphin Island was a beach town, practically a resort compared to other places we had stayed. All the houses were on stilts, and white beaches were everywhere. Just checking into our hotel I felt like I was on vacation. At least until we got into our room. The hotel's exterior was a gorgeous two story dream of white walls and a wooden sidewalk. The mid afternoon breeze carried the sounds of singing birds and crashing waves. For that moment my day was heavenly. And then it was all gone as soon as I stepped into our room. From the art to the carpet, it was just like every other hotel I've ever been in. Nice but nothing special. Nice the way boring can be regarded as pleasant. Just another king size bed and four walls schemed to the tune of tope. And the first thing The Boss did to get comfortable was strip naked and say, "I'm gonna shower. You get the laundry. Tell whatever Chinawomen runnin' the place to go light on the starch. I wanna look m'best."

So I found us a Laundromat. I actually had to leave the island and head north into another town, but I found one. I went through my usual routine of asking the locals about the town, the nightlife, and good places to meet people. I got coffee, a book of crosswords, and found a quiet place on the coast to sit, watch the waves, and pretend I was living a different life. As far as fantasies go, I could've done worse. I pictured my parents, pretending my father was still alive. I imagined us all living in a small, cobble brick town with cafés and bakeries stocked with fresh bagels every morning. Somewhere in there I'd meet a nice girl and in winter we'd go snowboarding. We'd spend our nights dancing in small clubs, or drinking wine on our balcony. We'd volunteer at an animal shelter and have a collie, even though I'm allergic. After all, as long as I was daydreaming, I figured I might as well dream big. So between the fantasy, the smell of my coffee, and the breeze mingling with the waves, for just moment I back on vacation. At least until my cell phone started to vibrate.

"*Millie!*" The Boss screamed on the other end. "*Millie! When in the ass crack of time are m'pants gonna be done? I been freezin' in this 'ere petite fuckin' hotel robe, polishin' Daisy Duke and dripping shower water off m'balls fer the past two hours! Where the hell are you? No! Don't bother. I don' give two shits. Jus' gitch-er dainty, dykin' ass back here. Now!* "

A thing about The Boss is, he names all his guns. *Daisy Duke* is a sawn-off double barrel shotgun with thirty seven notches down the length of the barrel. To call it his favorite would be an understatement.

I have to admit, round three with The Boss's pecker was an amusing sight. A little disturbing, but he wasn't lying about his attire. I had to laugh. Two steps back into the room and my fearless leader was towering over me in an open bathrobe, about ten sizes too small. He was yelling so hard that all the muscles in his chest were twitching, which in turn was making his belly jiggle. The veins in his neck and temples seemed ready to burst as he chewed me out, and all I could do was think about how I'd left the air conditioning on all afternoon. Standing before me was a naked grizzly bear of a man, threatening every kind of violence imaginable. And there I was, trying not to laugh at how the cold had shriveled his pecker. By the time he punched the wall and the bitty thing bounced, I lost it. I couldn't control myself. He may have kept yelling, but I was laughing too hard to notice.

A thing about The Boss is, he's the worst man alive and he knows it. For the rest of the world, he doesn't care. For me, he has something of a soft spot. By the time he had dressed, his temper had died and he offered to buy me a new crossword book, even though the one I'd just purchased was in plain sight on the table. "We can find us a magazine stand or somethin' an' getch you one of them puzzle books you like so much. A good one. Like from the New York Times. Maybe even some o' them dyke mags. At least those we can share."

Ever since I told him I was a lesbian, he can't shake the belief that I must enjoy magazines like *Penthouse* and *Hustler*. I've tried to explain to him that the women in those magazines are fake and exploited, but such ideas are beyond him.

"*Now* hold up a minute there. Suffrage of the straight dames ended since what? Was the forties, right? Ain't nobody been exploited since that Rodney guy got his negro ass clubbed upside the head. That was uh, well o'er a decade ago. At least."

"God damn it, Gus!" It's funny how he can yell all day and I can keep my frustration inside. The minute he tries to be civil and have a conversation, he says the wrong thing and I've finally had enough. For the most part it's just who he is and the life I chose. But then there's the little stuff. Sometimes I just can't stomach the little stuff.

"I told you about The Lord's name, missy," he snaps back. "Shit, I told you 'bout my name besides! I don' wanna hear it from you no more!"

"I told you nobody says '*negro*!' Nobody! And people are exploited every day, in the worst of ways. How can you consistently pretend to remain so naive? It's the gay marriage conversation all over again!"

He snorts a little laugh when I say, "*gay marriage*," and then tries to pass it off like a cough. He knows which buttons not to push. I know which ones he likes to push anyway. And for that, I can't help but want to unload *Daisy Duke* at his face. Not that it'll get me anywhere.

"I thought I ain't supposed to say *nigger*."

"Either!" I stamp my foot. "You know they're both horrible words. Nobody says *negro*. Nobody says *nigger*. They're the worst words, anywhere. You just don't use them! And while we're on the subject, *Chinawoman at the Laundromat*? " Even as I yell, I know it isn't the last time we'll be having this conversation. In the back of my head, I give him two weeks, maybe three. As much as I hate it, he couldn't care less about the rest of the world. Strangers are just soulless entities, wandering aimlessly and occasionally getting in his way. Like flies. So who cares what he calls them?

"And you don't say peep 'bout God," he stands up and points, jabbing his finger at my collarbone. The instant it makes contact, the instant his finger taps me hard enough that I have to take a step back and rebalance myself, his expression changes. It was an accident.

Not that it stops me from yelling back. "You're hitting me now?" I scream and storm into the bathroom. I slam the door behind me and catch sight of myself in the mirror. I'm already crying, which makes me even angrier because I hate how he gets to me. More than anything, I hate that. I hate being his chauffer. I hate running his errands. I hate how he sees the world. I hate how small minded he is, and cruel. And self serving. More than anything, I hate how I can't just let myself feel numb around him.

So I cry. I sit on the edge of the bathtub and take off my stupid, fat, black glasses. I let myself let it out, but not loud enough for him to hear. I try to think about other things, just to keep myself calm. I think about my parents. I remember growing up on the base. I think of college and how things like converting to moles used to be exciting. Then for no reason, I start thinking about how skinny I am and how I liked my hair when it was longer, but don't have the patience to grow it out again. Then I start thinking about running The Boss over with his truck.

That actually helps a little.

A few minutes go by and The Boss knocks on the bathroom door. "Millie?" he asks, as if I might not be in here. "Millie? Look, I didn't mean that. Well, no. I meant ta point. I meant to be aggressive. But I got carried away and I didn't mean ta actually touch ya. I know- I know how all ya'll fuckin' dykes hate men touching ya. It's like a damned sickness fer yer kind, and for that, well…I- I shouldn't've gotten all carried away is all."

After a considerable silence, he lightly knocks on the door again. "The thing of it is, Millie, you know I only got one saving grace in me. Even if there ain't no redemption, I ain't never spoke unkindly of The Lord and I ain't never tolerated it neither. Far as that goes, I gotta be firm. I may burn forever in Hell, but at least I'll burn with that ounce of pride. That don' make what I did right, but- you know.

"And, hey, remember how ya told me to talk 'bout my feelings? You know, recognize what I'm doin' n' feelin' n' shit? Well, here's me, talkin' 'bout the wrong I done. I ain't stormin' off, getting' wasted, and fuckin' the nearest thing I can get on all fours. I ain't shootin' up the place. I ain't even burned nothin.' I'm just doin' like ya told me and talkin' about and knowin' what I did and what ain't right about it."

Another bit of silence creeps by and he smacks the door hard enough to make everything on the bathroom counter rattle. "Damn it, Millie! We got a fuckin' job to do and this shit don' get it done. You fuckin' hear me in there? – No. Shit. Damn it! - This ain't right o' me neither! We got a job to do. I'm gonna go start hittin' up the karaoke bars. You get yer shit together. You call me. You find me. I don' think nothin'll happen to me on this one, but there ain't no promises. I need to know you got my back. I left *Tom* and *Huck* locked and loaded on the table for ya. The batteries in them laser sights is fresh. The knives and guns is loaded n' re-stashed in the truck. *Daisy Duke*'s between them mattresses. I'm keepin' a couple other pieces in the truck, but I'll be unarmed. You get yer shit together n' you call me!" Then he punches the door again and screams, "Fuck!" He leaves and I'm left to wonder how much of what he said was true and how much was just to get me out of the bathroom.

A thing about The Boss is, he gave all my guns boy names. He even put laser sights on all of them because he believes that girls can't aim. The day I woke up to him calibrating the stupid things, he even said he was, "makin' 'em dainty," for me.

And yes, even my twelve gauge scattergun, *Queequeg*, has a laser sight.

Another thing about The Boss is, he was born in Georgia, but has actually lived all around the world. His accents come and go and change every couple of weeks. We entered Alabama; he started dropping his G's. It's anyone's guess as to why. Nobody else around here seems to do it.

I take my time calling him. As long as he's in a panic over me not being at his side, I might as well savor it. Most of the time I feel like The Boss can do without me anyway. Besides, we aren't even sure this is the place. Granted, he's been that much more of a bully today. Somehow that's always been a sign. The closer we are to danger, the more macho he becomes. It's like he has a sixth sense for the hunt. But on the other hand, we've been following these missing person's reports up and down the coast for nearly two months. We've heard rumors. We've had a fairly solid theory of what we're after. But to be certain that tonight's the night?

I'm in no hurry. Besides, Mama used to say there wasn't a problem in the world a hot bath couldn't cure. After dealing with The Boss all day, I decide I deserve one. I even try for bubbles using the hotel shampoo, but it doesn't get me far. A few suds come up, but are gone by the time I wet my hair. And then it isn't long before I start to feel bored. I would read or pick at a crossword, but I've never trusted myself holding paper over water. Just sitting there, knowing the hunt is on and maybe, for once, The Boss might be in over his head, I decide I have to forgive him. At least a little. For now.

"You were right, Mama," I whisper to myself. The bath helped. At least until I notice myself in the mirror. At the sight of my body, I decide I look something like a sick cat that's just come in from the storm. Twiggy, pale, and earning a belly from my on-the-road diet. I used to think of myself as a strong, beautiful person. Now, if not for the tattoos I wouldn't even recognize myself. Even my hair looks broken. Or more like a soggy haystack left to rot a few inches over my shoulders.

Of course, I wouldn't be traveling with The Boss if I didn't have a few scars. A couple bite and claw marks on my right shoulder and neck are the bad ones. A poorly stitched slash across my thigh from a knife, from the night I met Gus, is the only other that really stands out. Maybe the ones on my back, but I always forget about them.

And then there are my tattoos. I take a quick inventory as I dry myself. On my left foot I have a black toe tag, complete with a string inked around my big toe. From the fingers of my left hand, all the way up to my shoulder, I have around ninety little blue stars. Most of them are five pointed, but two of them have six. Those are for my parents. As for the rest of them, I honestly can't remember how many I have total. Whenever I feel like some new ink and I just don't know what to get, I have a few stars added. So I think it's about ninety. Then on that same shoulder, but more on my back, there's one of those monkeys from the *Barrel of Monkeys* game I had as a kid. Its one paw wraps just a little over my shoulder and he hangs there all day. Then I have a little, green and purple grape vine going up my left earlobe. Eventually I want to get something huge on my back. I can just never decide what.

I look over myself in the mirror and nod. Sometimes a little breathing is all I need. Now I can deal with The Boss. And right on cue, for the second time today, I hear my cell phone vibrate. A part of me is impressed. Another part is saddened that he's really getting the hang of outgoing calls. I make a note to buy him a phone with smaller keys. That'll stop his fat fingers.

I answer the call with, "Yeah, boss?"

"Shit, girl! How did ya know it was me?" He seems genuinely surprised. In the background I hear music and chatter. He must've found a place.

"The phone says your name," I sigh. "Also you're the only person I know."

"Phones actually tell you people's names now? Like, if I hand it over to this spick fuck-stick sitting down the bar a-ways, will the phone actually tell you it's 'Pablo Pablo' or somethin'?" For as long as I've known The Boss, I still can't decide whether he thinks he's being funny or is just that stupid.

Another man's voice comes through the line, *"Hey! Hey! What the fuck did you just call me?"*

"Oh, hang on, Millie. I gotta pacify me the locals." There's a short pause.

"I asked you a question, faggot! What the fuck did you just call me?"

"I called you a worthless Mexican fuck-stick too dead to save his girlfriend from the facial raping of a lifetime. Now what are you going to do about it?"

-A significantly longer pause-

"Hey, barkeep," the other man's voice yells. *"Whatever this man's drinking tonight. It's on me."*

"And the drinks for my fuckin' dyke friend, whenever she gets here."

"Oh, of course. –Barkeep, drinks for some, uh, some lesbian too, I guess."

"Boss?" I snap. "Boss!"

"Good news, Millie," He says. *"We're drinking free tonight. Not too much for you though. We gotta job to do."*

"Boss?" I start fishing around the hotel room for my clothes. The urgency to sprint out the door and control him overwhelms me. Still, I take the time to scold him. "Did you just glamour that man?"

"Hypnotize, Millie. Hypnotize. I won't abide none of that sissy vampire speak while I'm drinkin'. Anyways, you get down here soon enough and we'll have a toast to a hunt nearly over. I think I'm gazin' upon our targets as we speak."

I freeze. "They're there? How many? Are you sure it's them?"

"Three, and I can smell 'em. There's definitely somethin' different 'bout these girls. Somethin' sweet."

"Okay, okay! I'm on my way." I dive through my bag, digging out the first clean top and pair of shorts I can find. Had I not been so rushed, I likely would've done better than corduroy short-shorts and a baggy, tie dye mess of a t-shirt, but I'm not thinking. I snatch up my glasses, slap on a belt, and holster *Tom* and *Huck* to the small of my back.

"*You don't even know where I am.*"

"No, it's okay. Just leave your phone on and I'll follow its GPS."

"*I'm at Paulo's Karaoke Club. Did you say this phone's got a Jeep in it?*"

I pause. I can't help but want to slam my head against the wall. "Yeah, boss. Your phone has a Jeep signal, and I can use it to track you," I say before hanging up. Shaking my head, I take a moment to look in the bathroom mirror and make sure my guns aren't showing. Dated and hideous as the shirt may be, at least it's functional. I still debate for half a second on changing into something else, but decide I'm here for work. It's okay to look entirely lame. So at that I pick up my hotel key, take two steps out the door, and realize I'm not going anywhere.

Of course The Boss took the truck.

It takes a while before I'm able to walk into the bar. After the cab ride from hell, I have to breathe outside for a few minutes, find a dark corner of the parking lot and dry heave. Eventually I work up the nerve to make my way inside and cringe to the sound of three tramps on stage hitting all the whole notes flat. I look them over and decide they're nothing but a bunch of cleavage. Like a bad joke, they stand in the order of blonde, brunette, and redhead. Their outfits consist of sparkly tank tops with blue jeans on one and pleated skirts on the others. Their eye shadow is so thick, in this light I could mistake them all for victims of physical abuse.

I stop myself. I try to think of a funnier remark about their make-up than being beaten, but I can't. Shaking my head, I watch the singing tramps. At least, I decide the red head and brunette look trampy. The blonde is actually quite pretty, even if her make-up borders along Halloween mask territory. So I stare for a moment, but their singing is so irritating, I start scanning the audience for The Boss. If I'm lucky he already has our prey close to him so we can hurry up and get out of here. But I don't see him. And as I look out at all the faces in the crowd, I'm a little thrown by how quiet everyone is. I mean, even with three tramps attempting to sing on stage, it's hard to believe that nobody in this bar is talking.

Wait. Why do I keep calling them tramps? I roll my eyes and log the micro aggression as a side effect of having spent far too much time with The Boss. Little by little, he keeps eroding away everything I like about myself.

"*Psssst!* Millie!" The Boss attempts a whisper from a high table near the bar, all the way at the far side of the room. Given how loud he normally is, his voice still carries like he's standing next to me. "Millie! Over here! Millie! *Psst*!"

He gets louder, so I wave to silence him. I continue watching the audience as I walk back and can't help but feel somewhat fascinated at how everyone is entirely silent. Every face, every set of eyes is transfixed on stage. Wow, I think. These… extroverted women in attire suitable for a night out in Alabama's heat… these women are *really* terrible to shut everyone up like this. Nobody is even booing. Maybe it's like they're all watching a train wreck or something. They want to look away but just can't help themselves. Granted, as my eyes adjust to the dark, I notice a lot of the men's jaws are agape. Some of the women are glaring at their husbands and boyfriends, blatantly annoyed. I even catch some lady look from the girls on stage down to her own chest. She adjusts her tank top, but sighs in bitter disappointment.

"Ain't they beautiful?" The Boss points his beer toward the stage as I sit in an adjacent stool. He doesn't even think to look at me and I can imagine the derangement of sex acts playing through his thoughts as his gaze drifts from one girl's curves to the next.

"Stunning," I say. "But don't you think you should be distinguishing them by their personalities and judge them based on character?"

"Yeah," he nods and speaks in a whisper. "You're right, Millie. That must be it. They *do* seem like true ladies of character. They prob'bly got themselves a hundred virtues each I ain't never even known."

I look back at the stage. Even from the far side of the room I can't help but feel like I'm peering into the burgundy end of a red light district. A high note comes into whatever song the trio is murdering and one of them screams like an injured child.

"You ever heard such music?" Gus continues to whisper. Not just a quiet whisper. More like he's captivated. He speaks in that soft tone people use over sunsets when the meaning of life seems perfectly clear. "*You ever heard such music*?" like he's speaking for a choir of angels instead of what might as well be the three little pigs running scared through traffic.

"Doesn't quite compare to that porcupine you kicked last month," I say.

"Ain't a sound in the natural world to compare to this," he says. "I'm glad ya got here in time ta experience it."

"About that," I say. "Do you have any idea what I went through on the cab ride here?" He doesn't seem to respond, so I say something to snap him out of it. "Your wife was driving," I try, and he doesn't react. Normally the mention of Gretchen is enough to make him at least draw a knife or threaten to injure me. But The Boss just tilts his head, never taking his eyes off the stage. "We were in a fatal car wreck," I say. "I should be dead right now. Again."

Another screech comes from the stage and The Boss whispers, "Why'd I ever give up on man? There's still some good in the world, ain't there?"

"Oh my-" I clasp my hands over my mouth before I can say the G word. Such speech from The Boss is unheard of. "You're on drugs right now, aren't you?"

"Sorry, Millie. The song has me lost over m'ways. I ain't never heard *Bad, Bad Leroy Brown* with such *perferzionamento*[1]."

"Which song?"

The screeches and squeals interpreted as singing come to a halt and all the men in the place are on their feet. Applause strikes like cannon fire, underscored throughout the crowd with hoots and whistles of the lowest caliber. Even The Boss's hands are stretched out over his head, clapping thunder as he lets out a couple of wolf-like howls.

---

[1] Italian for *perfection*. I think. Maybe it was French.

In the calamity of cheering I hear several women's voices.

"Oh my god, we are so leaving!"

"Dale? Dale? Dale! Do you hear me, Dale?"

"Are you serious? On our anniversary?"

As I look into the crowd I see several more women yelling at their husbands and boyfriends. They're being ignored. All their men are standing, applauding the *singers* like they're offering blow jobs and tax breaks to whoever makes the most noise. They're all entranced. Enchanted.

"Boss!" I scream. "Boss?"

"Yeah, Millie?" He answers without looking. He continues to applaud.

"Are you in control?" I ask.

"Think so," he shrugs his shoulders and whistles toward the stage after one of the girls curtsies and her skirt rides a little high.

It all sinks in. Their singing captivates all the men. Three girls. The Boss said there were three on the phone. "Oh, come on!" I say. "Them? They're the ones killing and cannibalizing men?"

The Boss bobbles his head. As the applause in the room dies down, he settles and takes a hard swig of his beer. "Well, it ain't quite cannibalism, but yeah. Gotta be," he says. "They smell sweet. In a hunderd n' fifty years, I ain't never heard voices like theirs. And not jus' any pack a wild bitches'll sing-fuck a room to madness."

I sniff the air and all I detect is a war between beer, sweat, and a hundred kinds of cologne. I look back at the stage. An emcee in a glittery suit comes on and says, "All right! All right! That was Thelma, Angie, and Penny, blessing us all with the stylings of Mister Jim Croche! Lets give these lovely and talented ladies another big round of applause!" Again, the clapping and cheers from the crowd are deafening. "Few people know this," the emcee carries on, "but the song was originally written about an old army buddy of Croche's. Seems he was a big, bad man who went AWOL but still came back for his paycheck. I think we can all understand that in this economy!" I'm uncertain if the emcee is attempting humor, but he's the sort of entertainer I can't help but feel embarrassed to be in the same room as. "So to get our mind off our financial troubles, here's..." he trails off, taking a moment to view an index card in his hand. “Here’s Marc Rumsfeld and Quinn Foster with, um, David Bowie’s *Suffragette City*.”

A portly man and bitty waif of a girl take the stage to little interest of the audience. Most of the men are still transfixed on the three sirens stepping off the far side of the stage. From the back of the room, I hear several of them offer to purchase the trio drinks.

The Boss is chugging his beer in one hand and holding a pitcher in the other, ready to refill his conviction to tonight’s hunt. “Ya know, Millie,” he says with froth dripping down his beard. “You could take a lesson from them hellions. Maybe if you dressed up a bit pertier you’d get some more attention. Why, I bet if ya’ll got dolled up on occasion, you’d prob’bly even find yerself a man and wouldn’t have to work so hard at dyke’n all the time.”

I remain calm. I don’t break the pitcher over his head. “Do I really have to explain genetics again?” I ask with my teeth clenched. “It’s not a choice. Or even if it is, I’m happy with decision I’m naturally compelled toward.”

“Sure,” he chuckles and tugs on the shoulder of my t-shirt until it snaps back at me. “I’m jus’ sayin,’ I know squat about clothes and even I’m certain tie dye shat itself outta style thirty years ago.”

I don’t break the pitcher over his head. “So how do you want to do this?” I ask, nodding toward the sirens. In the front of the room, they’re already surrounded by a gaggle of horny college boys. Some of them are coaxing the girls to sing again, despite the underrated duo on stage putting their hearts into Bowie.

“Well, once the job’s over I s’pose we ought to find ourselves a sort of dress shop. Then we spend the better part of the afternoon findin’ outfits suggestive to the idea of you packin’ some real tits in that two grape valley you call a chest.”

I break the pitcher over his head. At least, in my heart I feel myself breaking a pitcher over his head. In my mind’s eye I picture the glass scraping his face and alcohol stinging the wounds. But really I just give him a stink eye and snap a whisper of, “The job! How do you want to do the job?”

“Oh,” he shrugs and glances over at the women, surrounded by men. From the way his eyes travel, I can tell he's playing out a little fantasy in his head. "Nothin' to it. You just wait at the bar. I lure them over, put a few rounds in 'em, and talk them toward someplace quiet. If evry-thins right about these sirens, they'll try n' kill me n' eat m'flesh. You follow along. When they try fer killin' me, you start shootin' and I'll start shootin' and that'll be that. Make sure I've sealed the deal, but leave ahead of us. Get by the truck incase you need to drive. Wait for us to come out and follow along. That's the plan."

"What?"

"Yep. I suspect findin' them was the hardest part. The rest of tonight'll be easy. Messy, I think. But it's smooth sailing from here. I just got to send the right vibes their way, ya know."

To say I'm dumbfounded is an understatement. "Are you joking?"

"Didn't laugh, did I?"

"With all the men drooling over these girls, how could you possibly expect them to give you a single glance?"

He laughs. He snorts his nose hard enough to make his moustache hairs stand on end. "Men?" He takes an amused glance around the bar and says, "There ain't been a real man born since before the Second World War. Maybe the fifties at best, but only 'cause I been drinkin' and it has me feelin' generous. What passes for a man these days…" He trails off into a couple gulps of beer. "Truth is, Millie, your generation and every one to follow is too damn full o' itself to mold real men. Ya'll just becomin' bigger n' bigger kids. And them ladies over there," he points his glass to the sirens. "Them ancient an' beautiful creatures o'er there been pickin' at scraps the past half century. They spot an entrée the size a' me and their mouths'll be waterin' n' no time. Shit, I'll have their nethers droolin' by the time I learn their names."

"As if you'd bother to learn their names," I say. "And! And as if you of all people would know anything about what makes a man!"

He chuckles a bit. "So the barely legal clit licker thinks she's wise in years enough to know a thing about manhood? Millie, get yer bony ass over to the bar and pay attention. I'll learn ya somethin.'"

"Fine," I say. I demand the truck keys and he hands them over. "Right. Either we'll follow them with whatever poor sap they drag off tonight, or if by some miracle they actually willingly approach your table, I'll keep my distance but follow you around."

"And you leave ahead of us."

I glance across the room at the girls drinking with a couple of college boys, giggling and tossing their hair. "Sure," I say. "Whatever."

A thing about The Boss's keys is that his keychain is a souvenir bottle opener from the Narita Airport in Tokyo, Japan. If asked, The Boss claims to have never once flown in his life. I know this isn't true though. He flew the night I met him.

I sit at the bar and decide to spoil myself with a Coke. "We got Pepsi," The bartender says in what feels like an accusatory tone. I can't decide if it's just me feeling frustrated or if he's actually offended that I'd order a soft drink over something stiff. Either way, I nod and fake a little smile.

He gets my drink.

I stare at the back of the bar. Beyond the bottles and hanging glasses is an enormous mirror that actually gives me a pretty good view without having to turn around. On one side I can watch The Boss, drinking alone. On the other side I can see clear across the room. I have a perfect view of the sirens receiving praise from a small horde of would-be-suitors.

I watch both scenes closely.

On one side there are shots being raised. Some young dope with a cigarette is championing one of the girl's on his shoulder as she raises her glass to her, "Sisters!" A dozen other glasses are raised to hoots and whistles. Everybody drinks and everybody laughs.

On the other side, The Boss drinks alone.

I look at my Pepsi and sigh. I know it's going to stain my teeth. I know it's going to shred the lining of my stomach. And yes, I know how bloated I'm going to feel after another one or two of these.

I sip from the straw. Even though it's not Coke, it still is beautiful.

Half an hour goes by and I'm starting to get bored. At one point the sirens returned to the stage and butchered all eight and a half minutes of *Purple Rain* with much cheer from the crowd. Down the bar I hear an older man say, "Shit, I never knew Prince could sound like sex!" and have to laugh.

Crazy old man. Prince *is* sex.

But even with that little amusement, I can't help but wonder if tonight is even going anywhere. Through the mirror, on one side of me life is a party. On the other, The Boss is drinking alone. In all this time he hasn't so much as lifted his head or ordered another pitcher. He just sits over his half empty glass, watching the beer inside like it's telling a story. He doesn't look to me. He doesn't look to the crowd. He just sits and drinks at his own pace.

I start to wonder when he's going to make a move. Not that I'm expecting much, but what's he waiting for? Every minute he sits there doing nothing is another the girls continue to play at the hearts and libidos of every other man in the place. In a crowd this size, it'll take no time for them to pick their next victims. And yet, The Boss does nothing. But why? Why?

By my third Pepsi it's really bothering me. I start to hypothesize that this is his angle. This is his entire scheme. We've theorized that the women have been picking up men who are alone, so he's playing some sort of loneliest-man-on-earth routine. But that can't be right because he'd been talking about impressing the women with his macho, macho manliness. Hunched over a dark table doesn't exactly stand out in a crowd. So what's he doing? What's his plan? What is he thinking?

"What are you drinking?" a smoker's voice says next to me. When I glance over I see I've been joined by saggy looking man with sunken eyes and a bad shave. I know he's a creep by the toothpick dancing between his lips.

"Alone," I say. "I'm drinking alone."

"Heh," he says a laugh and scoots himself onto the stool next to mine. "Well, I got something spicier you should try."

"Look," I start to say.

"Oh I am," he says. "Believe me. I've been looking since you walked into the place. But don't you worry though. I'm not one of those scumbags you hear about all over television. You know. The kind who prey on sexy little things like yourself. I'm actually a real classy guy. A citizen of the world, you might say. Carl. You can call me Carl."

"Are you for real?" I lean away as he nudges himself a bit closer. "Look," I raise my voice. "I'm sure you're a very cultured man but I'd like to be left alone."

"Oh you're shy, aren't you? I get that. I get that!" his breath smells of whiskey and menthol and I can see sweat stains when he lifts his arm to signal the bartender. Without breaking stride he continues, "But ever since you walked in here I've been feeling like you and I have this sort of connection. Like maybe soulmates or some shit. Ever since you walked in here, I've been feeling like my whole purpose in this world is to become one with you."

I start to stand up, to back away, but Carl reaches out to grab my waist. The only thing is, once he grabs me, he realizes it's not the small of my back he's touching. It's the handle to a .45mm USP named *Huck.*

Carl freezes, looking into my eyes. I can see myself in them.

That's right, I think. This girl's packing some serious heat. Now you know. Just walk away.

He stares me down.

I slowly nod.

"You carrying a piece?" he laughs and throws up my shirt enough to snatch the gun out of its holster.

"No!" I scream, but it's too late. He has my *Huck* and is waving it loosely around the room.

"Holy shit," he says with a small chuckle. "This thing loaded, Millie?" He cocks it and aims toward wherever. He starts to pull the trigger, but his wrist is limp so the gun angles toward me.

A shot fires.

I jump.

The entire room jumps.

Carl lets out a blood curdling scream.

When I look, The Boss is holding Carl up by the wrist, poising the gun toward the ceiling. A little dust and plaster rains down on them. "Drop the pistol," he says clearly, dropping his latest accent and taking on the commanding force of an army general.

Carl writhes in the air, screaming, "My hand! My hand!"

"You can have it back when you let go of the gun," He speaks down to Carl. His tone takes me back to being a little a girl, and the way my Dad used to yell at me as a kid.

Carl continues to scream. I hear a snap and his face turns purple. "My hand!"

The Boss lowers Carl but doesn't let go. He instead looks quizzically at the hand he's holding, which is also turning deep purple. "Why, I reckon I broke your wrist there," he says. "That's what you get for playing with guns, I guess." The Boss then grabs *Huck* with his free hand and pries it from Carl's fingers. He then sets the gun on the bar next to me and says, "Are you all right, ma'am."

He speaks to me like a stranger. Suddenly I forget about my childhood and instead remember how Dad and I used to talk when I was teen. I give a little nod and note the nearest exit.

"Well, good then. It sure would've ruined everyone's evening if you lost your face to a bullet."

A few random people chuckle.

The Boss looks smug as can be. The entire place is watching us. The patrons. The emcee. The three sirens. And he's just so tickled with himself for it. He lifts Carl at arms length like a soiled diaper and says, "Well, uh, let's say we show him the door, shall we!" Well, a soiled diaper or a trophy.

Everyone cheers.

The Boss marches Carl toward the door to the tune of a standing ovation from the crowd. And then it dawns on me. Just a minute ago, right before Carl fired my gun, he said my name. He said, "*This thing loaded, Millie?*" He knew me. And he went for my gun.

This was all a set up.

The Boss must've put my image into Carl's head before I arrived. He made Carl believe he was in love with me, or at least lusting after me. And then he filled the little creep's mind with all the right things to say. Everything that would push a button. Then all he had to do was sit back and wait. Carl worked up the nerve to talk to me, unknowingly went for my gun, and The Boss was conveniently there to save the day. Suddenly he's everyone's hero. He marches Carl out the door with a crowd of three quarters of the room gathering behind him. They all go into the parking lot and just about everyone left gathers at the door.

From outside I hear The Boss call out, "Say, who's got some rope?"

There's cheering, hooting, and laughter. I rub my temples under my glasses and order another Pepsi. About ten minutes goes by and smiling faces start filtering back into the bar. Everyone's amused. Everyone's having the time of their lives. And then in walks The Boss with his arms over the shoulders of all three sirens.

"You're kidding me," I utter to myself.

Even worse, every full glass in the place gets raised in his direction. "To Gus!" someone calls out.

"To Gus!" everyone yells before taking a hard chug. One of the sirens, the brunette, stands on her toes to kiss him on the cheek. Then the blonde yells, "Get this man some liquor!"

If I didn't already know the truth about Hell, I'd be convinced that I'd just landed in it.

"Shucks," The Boss says. "I just came in for some music and a quiet drink to myself. I just done like what any of you woulda. If ya'll saw it."

By the time he's finished faking humbleness, the bartender hands him a full pitcher and says, "Well, you aren't drinking alone anymore."

Everyone cheers again and The Boss holds the pitcher over his head like a trophy before taking a hard drink that spills onto his beard and chest. Of course everyone cheers to this as well.

It occurs to me that despite everything I know, there very well may be two Hells. The regular one and Paolo's Karaoke Club. Or maybe the imps and demons of Hell built this place especially for me. Yes, that could be it. I died in the taxi on the way to meet The Boss, and now I'm in my own private chamber of Hell where there's no Coke, Prince is continuously murdered with his own music, and The Boss is regarded as a champion and distinguished gentleman.

No. No. I deflate my sense of self importance.

Sometimes I'm just in Alabama.

With the pace of the evening set, it continues as expected. For a short while a bulk of the crowd surrounds The

Boss and sirens at their table. The celebration eventually starts to thin out. Within half an hour a lot of attention has returned to karaoke and people are distracted by a married woman on stage singing *Summer Love* from the *Grease* soundtrack.

At The Boss's table lies are being passed around as quick as the shots. They get each other's names honestly (for all I know), but the rest of their conversation is one piece of fiction after another.

The girls are Thelma, Angie, and Penny. According to their story they're all telecommunication majors at one of the local universities, out for a night on the town before buckling down for a week of studying and exams. They even referred to their college as "one of the local universities." I will give them credit though. Had it been me in their position, I would've said I was studying music theory, theater, or even theology. They could've pulled off being history majors, or even just said they were local dancers taking the night off. Anyway, name a college student who doesn't proudly state the name of her school.

As for The Boss, he's still Gus, but his last name has been changed to Johnson. No shock there. And instead of being a hunter on a quest of revenge, he explains himself as a former ranch hand who'd been laid off and widowed. I suppose there is a good deal of truth to that. It's just that those events happened well over a century ago. He also leaves out the bits of alcoholism, murderous rampages, and being an avid lover of farm animals. A very avid lover of farm animals.

"Oh my god," Angie cuts The Boss off in the middle of one of his stories. "I love your boots!"

"Thank you," The Boss says. "I made 'em m'self." He doesn't tell her what his boots are made of.

Angie is the brunette and has the personality and depth of a champagne bubble. Her cover story is that she grew up in Wisconsin where her father worked as a manager in a salt mine. She didn't have a lot of friends growing up, so she read and had a passion for listening to the radio. Hence the telecommunications. Or to put it another way, Angie has absolutely no idea what telecommunication majors do. To her advantage, The Boss really wouldn't know anything about it either. Granted, he knows she's lying to him. It's just that he's probably a lot more impressed with her stories than I am.

"I really like your eyes," The Boss says.

“Oh, stop,” Angie fakes modesty while batting her lashes. If any of them were to look through the mirror at the bar, they’d catch my eyes rolling.

A thing about The Boss is he’s thick. Real thick. He may know they’re lying. He may already be entertaining fantasies of disemboweling all three of these women. But he’s still a testosterone filled pervert of a man. A little wink from a kinky girl like that and lord knows where his mind will wander.

Standing across the table is Thelma, a redhead in a matching skirt. She doesn’t say much. She really doesn’t do much more than twirl her perfect curls of hair in one finger. Well, that and lean forward just enough to make everybody behind her think they’re about to get a free show. For a few minutes I let myself believe she’s the quiet, contemplative type. I imagine she’s watching The Boss, trying to determine how easy it’ll be to kill him. Or maybe she already has it all figured out and is currently pondering more important things. Like the meaning of life, climate change, or something along those lines.

Of course Thelma spoils this illusion the moment she opens her mouth.

The Boss is going on about how working on a farm is lonely, but a good and honest living with plenty of fresh air and beautiful sunsets. Somewhere in this, Thelma’s attempt to include herself in conversation is, “Well, I just adore chickens.”

I catch myself smirking in the mirror. Thelma isn’t quiet or contemplative. She’s not a deep thinker and she’s never going to solve global warming. She’s just dumb.

“Oh, uh,” The Boss tries to go along with it just the same. “We actually never had no chickens, but yeah. I s’pose they’re uh, well, they’re cute n’ their peckin.’ Kinda fluffy in a way. With feathers. I never really thought about ‘em before.”

“So you like feathers?” she asks

“Sure,” The Boss nods and gives me a brief glance through the mirror. Our eyes meet and The Boss’s mind invades my consciousness with the image of a redheaded short bus driving itself off a cliff. “Sure,” The Boss says again to Thelma. “Why not?”

The Boss had pointed out earlier how these women were ancient creatures. For all I know, they may be older than time itself. If this is true, I can't help but wonder how Thelma has lasted so many centuries without knowing how to have a proper conversation. Then again, The Boss has lasted well over a century and he's not exactly the brightest bulb on the tree. Of course he does have the advantage being able to rip out people's spines with his bare hands. And by that standard, Thelma does have her sisters to support her, along with bosoms the size of me.

It dawns on me that these people are the world's immortals. Brutes and tramps, dumb as dirt, lusting for blood, and they're the ones who will pass through the ages.

For a moment, I mourn over life's cruelty. I slam my Pepsi the way The Boss slams vodka. I curse myself for calling them tramps again and try to recall the days when I wouldn't even think to use that word. It stings knowing they really weren't so long ago.

The last of the sirens is Penny, the platinum perfect blonde. I hate to accept how drop dead gorgeous she is, but everyone else in the room has so why fight it? Even in her icing thick makeup, her allure would make Marilyn Monroe and Madonna hold a grudge. Looking at her makes me feel dumpy about myself. Especially in my stupid tie dye bag of a shirt. And the most astonishing part of it is how she sings like an injured rodent's plea for help, but when she speaks she has the low sultry voice I'd expect from a goddess. Toss in her wide, practically doll-like eyes and not-too-bronze tan and I truly, truly have to hate her.

While the other girls come off as bar trash, Penny is undoubtedly the type of collected, venomous killer The Boss always warns me about. Watching her at his table is like being absorbed into one of those nature programs about a hunter luring its prey in for the kill. She stands at just the right the angle for The Boss's eyes to drift between the delicate curve at the small of her back and the suggestively revealing neckline of her tank top. Her slender arm arches gracefully, combing her hair to one side so The Boss can continue his gaze up the length of her neck. She purses her lips before kissing a sip from her drink, and ever so slowly bats her viper green eyes as she nods, listening tentatively as The Boss relates his story about the time a fifteen point buck got wedged halfway through his windshield.

"You lifted it out with your bare hands?" She lingers on the word *bare*. "From how you lifted that man earlier, I knew you were strong, but wow!" She pushes down on his bicep and her doll eyes grow a little wider. "Oh my," she says, and then mouths the word *god*. "Your arms are like rocks."

On the other side of Gus, Thelma has her hand on his other arm and said, "It's like he wrestles bears for a living." She lingers on the word *bears*. It's not as effective. "Angie, you have to feel his arms!"

Through the mirror, I watch as all three sirens graze their fingertips along Gus, pushing into his biceps. I remember a time my mother told me that cats lick people not because they're being affectionate, but because they're tenderizing meat. I can't be certain, but I think the same thing is happening at The Boss's table.

"To be fair," The Boss says, "The buck was probably lighter than ol' Carl." He glances again in my direction. Our eyes meet and images of naked thighs, hickeys, some goat, bare breasts, and decades of drunken, stumbling sex are forced into my mind. As if knowing his intentions with all the women on Earth aren't bad enough. Now I actually have to see them in my thoughts. And then it occurs to me, what if their singing did get to The Boss? What if he is enchanted by them, completely lost to their magical off-key powers?

Little by little, the fear starts creeping into me. I think back to earlier tonight, when The Boss was yelling at me through the bathroom door. He said he needed me on this one. Since when does Gus need people? Maybe he realizes how much danger we're in. Maybe, for once, he's truly nervous. Maybe he's even scared.

Wait. Who am I kidding? If The Boss thought anything was truly threatening him, he'd just get an erection and start cheering on the approaching hell storm.

I look over at the table. I watch him grin and flirt with the sirens. As one of their hands grazes his leg my fears flop to certainties. We're doomed.

Penny takes a napkin and pats some sweat off her forehead and chest. "It's getting so warm in here," she says. "I must be drunk. And you don't even seem buzzed."

The Boss shrugs. "I'm a big fella," he says, jiggling his belly with both hands. "Maybe we should switch to somethin' stronger 'n beer." He starts to stand, but stumbles back. After a second of balancing, he smiles with his eyes shut and says, "Well, maybe nothin' *too* much stronger. You ladies hang on. I'll be right back."

He stumbles to the bar and leans on it a few feet away from me. "Hey there, li'l missssy," he says to me, loud enough for the sirens to hear. "Havin' any more trouble with that there pistol o' yours?"

"I can't believe you hypnotized Carl," I half whisper. "I could've been killed."

He shrugs and in a softer voice says, "I told ya I'd learn ya somethin'. Pretty soon we're gonna be gettin' on to phase two."

"Want me to wait outside? Get ready to follow?" I stick to the mission. I know enough not to expect an apology.

"Nah. I want this in a controlled space. I'm thinkin' we lure the girls back to our hotel room. And I still want you leavin' ahead of us. I want you to get back to the room, get some guns outta the truck and stash them 'round the place. Behind the nightstand n' shit. Then you hide in the closet and you wait."

"What? Why? What if they want to take you someplace else?"

"Then I'll do what's needin' to be done someplace else. Don't get me wrong. I'd sure prefer to have yer backup. That Penny girl? The leader, I think. Yeah, I'm pretty sure she aims to rip my heart out n' eat it in front o' me."

"Yeah, and what if she succeeds?"

"Worse comes to worse, it'll take a good five years to piece myself together again. Six or seven if they shit me out across different states. Just come after 'em another way is all."

"And if they kill me?"

"Then when the world ends I'll see ya in Hell, you fuckin' dyke."

Through the mirror, just past The Boss's shoulder I catch sight of perfect platinum blonde hair. "Gussy baby, what's taking so long?"

The Boss flops around and grins. "Heya Penny lady," he says through his teeth. "Fuckin' bartender's takin' his sweet ass time. Have you met this li'l lady? I saved her life earlier, ya know. From some drunken pistolier wannabe named Carl."

"I saw," she says. She doesn't bother to look at me. I decide that if any shooting has to go down, I'm going to aim for her first. "You were amazing. That buffoon didn't stand a chance."

"Nobody e'er does," The Boss shrugs. Then he turns to me and starts putting on a show. "Anyways, I appreciate you offerin' to buy me and my lady friend's next round," he says. "Ya sure as shit don't have to, but the thought's appreciated."

I go along with it. "Please," I say. "I insist. You saved my life. You just order whatever you like and the next round is on me. You and all your lady friends."

Penny leans against the bar and says, "Now, that's awful kind of you," still without looking at me. She then calls down the bartender, "Hey! Hey, do you know how to make a Flaming Homer?"

The bartender nods with the dorkiest grin imaginable. I have to admit, I'm pretty impressed to. I never knew it was an actual drink.

Penny smiles. "Four Flaming Homer's and another pitcher of Amber Bock. And put them on her tab," she says, pointing at The Boss's table and then me. She then turns to Gus and says, "Shall we then?"

"I'll jus' be one second," Gus says. "I just wanna make sure this li'l lady here's gonna be all right."

"Such a gentleman," she smiles, grazing her fingernails along his back. Finally she turns to me and the smile vanishes. Our eyes lock and in the back of my mind I see the image of myself being ripped in half by a Cyclops. The image shifts to ones of The Boss. She's fantasizing about sucking the muscles off his cooked fingertips and using his bones for some bracelet she's making. "Thanks for the drinks," she sneers. Then she snaps back to playful, winking at The Boss and saying, "Don't take too long."

She walks back to their table. I can't help but take in all the sass she puts into her hips. When I glance at The Boss, I can tell he's enjoying the same view. He doesn't blush, but I can tell he's a little embarrassed. We both turn back to face the bar.

"She is evil," I say.

"Vicious," The Boss agrees. "A real monster."

"The way she came over here to stake her claim?"

"Like a wild dog. Get too close to her food and you'll lose a hand."

I nod. "I noticed. I saw it in her thoughts."

The Boss looks down at me, a little perplexed. "That's still happening?" he asks. "When you look in people's eyes?"

"Ever since I was bit," I shrug. I don't really think about it but my hand still comes up and rests itself over the scars on my shoulder. I feel the little bumps through my shirt and can't help but hate the world for a moment.

"Shit," The Boss says. "You never mention it. I guess I figured it wore off."

"There's a lot I don't mention," I sigh.

"Just as well," The Boss says. "I get sick o' yer voice sometimes anyway. Sure do appreciate you gettin' the laundry though. Anyways, maybe one day after we figure out how to kill the missus, things'll turn to normal for ya."

"Yeah," I nod. I look down at the ice in my glass. I think about calling my mother and letting her know I'm still alive. But I know I can't until this is all over. Until then she'll just have to settle for all the letters I keep writing and not sending. But I can't think about that. Not now. Tonight we have some sirens to kill. Maybe tomorrow we'll get back to more important things. "Anyway," I say. "Penny. Angie and Thelma. Are you sure you're up for this fight?"

"Ah, hell no," The Boss says, scratching his beard. "I'm so shitfaced right now. There ain't no way I can fight 'em. B'sides, I don't even want to think 'bout havin' to take them beautiful voices from this world."

"Gus!" I say a little louder than I should. Instantly I regret it because through the mirror, all three tramps snap their heads our way.

The Boss is quick to react. Even hammered, he seems to be in control. Loud enough for them to hear he says, "Hey, I was jus' offerin'. You bein' a fuckin' dyke an' all. I just figured maybe you oughta try a piece a cock before you go tits up all over town. But no worries. No worries at all. I got all sorts of beautiful ladies to entertain tonight. No reason I should give ya the charity when I got plenty to keep me up o'er there." He starts to stumble back toward the table, but then turns around and leans real close into me. I can smell half the bar in his breath. "Don't worry none," he whispers to me, grinning. "Jus' a few more drinks 'n I'll sober up while I fuck 'em. Then when they're all tired out n' got their guard down, that's when we make our move."

"Wait? What?"

"You heard the plan! I'm so hammered right now, I couldn't shoot straight if I tried. So I figure, we take 'em back to the room. The drive was –what, about an hour? So there's the drive. Then I'll screw the bunch, n' that'll be another while. They won't try to kill me until they think I'm too weak to fight back. So by the time I'm done fuckin' and they're all tired out, I'll be sober and we can make our move."

"You can't be serious."

"You got a better plan?"

"Yes! The original plan! That's disgusting!"

"It's the best plan I e'er made. I get some. You get too see some freaky dyke action prob'bly while I fuck them three back there. Then we get to kill them every way this side of Sunday. It's win-win all accounts."

"I don't enjoy killing! I do it because we have to. And you only planned this out because you want to sleep with them!"

"Like you don't. I saw you eyein' Miss Penny. First time I e'er understood why you're always dykin' so hard all the time."

"Boss, I am not leaving ahead of you so you can be lured off onto some backwoods road to be devoured. And I'm certainly not sitting in a closet while you have sex with those women."

"They ain't women, Millie. And you ain't got no choice. Now you get outta here, and I'll stall 'em another thirty minutes. If it makes you feel better, I'll have the bartender order us a cab and give the directions over the phone. That should settle things."

He heads back to the table. I take a few minutes to feel angry, settle my tab, and walk out.

A thing about The Boss is, he has a talent for making the bad days worse.

I take two steps into the parking lot and I realize I'm not going anywhere.

I have no idea where The Boss parked the truck. I see plenty of Fords, Dodge Rams, and SUVs. I see a beat up Golf, and what looks like a relatively new Porsche. I see a black Jetta with a box of crayons hanging from the rearview mirror. And no Boss's truck.

"Hello?" I think I hear a voice call. It's faint, but it sounded like someone called out, "Hello?"

Maybe it's the night I'm having, or about to have, but my first instinct is to draw *Tom* and *Huck* from their holsters. The parking lot curves around the building, so I walk slowly around, listening for another call. I peek my head around the corner. There are plenty of cars and vans sitting around. I see a Safari that looks like my mom's, but blue. I see two Jeeps, and for some reason this makes me want to smack The Boss upside the head. I see a classy Camaro that makes me wish I'd stayed in school. And chosen an education that would've actually lead to money.

"Hello?" I hear again. It's a man's voice. "Is anybody out there?"

I shrug. "I guess I'm out here."

"Hello?" The voice calls out, this time sounding a bit more frantic. "Who is that?"

"Who are you?"

"I'm Carl," he says.

Oh, jeez. It's Carl.

"Where are you?" Carl is calling out. "I can't see you."

"I'm not sure I want to see you," I call back.

"Please," he says. "I'm tied up. I don't know where I am. Although I think I'm behind Paulo's. Will you please help me?"

"You're behind the building?" I ask.

"Yeah," Carl keeps calling out. "Yeah, I'm tied up behind the building. Please come help."

I weigh my options. I slowly start making my way to the corner, guns aimed, and yell, "Carl? Do you see a pick up truck back there?"

"What?" Carl yells back. "Please, just help me! I'm tied up and I'm in a lot of pain."

"Please just answer my question, Carl. Do you see a pick up truck?" I slowly head toward the back of the lot, guns fixed in the general direction of Carl's voice.

"Damn it, lady! Please!" Then after a moment he says, "Wait! Wait! Is it a big, gray truck with red eyes painted on the hood? With a rust hole in the truck bed? And some steel boxes?"

Dang it! That is The Boss's truck. But I'm not so trusting. "What does the bumper sticker on the back say?"

"I can't see the back!"

I'm just about to the corner. "Fine. What's hanging from the mirror?"

"Please, I-I can't see windshield from here. I just need your help."

He can't see the back or the front? I step around the corner and then immediately regret that decision.

"Hey!" Carl screams, hanging upside down from a lamppost, directly above The Boss's truck. "Hey! There you are! Are you going to help me?" There's enough rope and cord around him that he looks like he's birthing from a cocoon. It's like his head just crowned out the bottom. "Oh my god, don't shoot me!" he yells.

I lower my guns. He's afraid of me, and therefore isn't under The Boss's spell. "I'm not going to shoot you," I say, walking up to the truck. "Do you remember how you got up there?"

He doesn't say anything for a moment. "No," he says. "No, ma'am, I don't. I remember driving here. We're at Paulo's, right?"

I nod. I walk up to the side of the truck. He's hanging directly above the bed. I gauge my distance to him if I was to climb onto the truck and untie him, but I don't think my arms can reach that far. I look around for a ladder or anything else tall, but there's nothing. "Why were you here?" I ask to keep him talking while I figure out what to do.

"I don't know. To get some drinks. Are you going to help me?"

"I'm not sure yet," I say. "Do you remember me at all?"

"What? No. Should I? The last thing I remember- the last thing was these three girls had come over to my table. They were flirting with me, I think. Yeah. They were flirting, and I figured they just wanted some free drinks. I was getting kind of sick of them so I asked if they were going to sing. I figured if they got on stage they'd leave me alone."

"You were getting sick of the three girls?" I smile. I look at all the ropes he's hanging by, and then the truck bed. He's directly above it. Maybe seven feet. Despite the rusty mess The Boss's truck is, the shocks are actually pretty good. "The blonde, brunette, and redhead? You didn't like them at all?"

Carl rolls his eyes. "No," he says. "The blonde was cute, but the other two just came off dumb. And I didn't want to be near women anyway. I'm- I'm going through a divorce. But I love my wife." He pauses for a moment. Hanging there, staring pitifully at me, I can see a tear roll down his forehead and get lost somewhere in his hair. "I just wanted to be left alone tonight. They went to sing, and then some big guy came up and- and I don't know after that."

The Boss saved his life. Gus must've seen the sirens around their prey and hypnotized him into falling for me. Then he set the stage to beat up Carl, proving himself as a more worthy meal.

"I don't know how I got here," Carl concludes to himself. "Please, will you help me down?"

"Sure, Carl," I say. "Just let me get my tool out of the truck." I fish the keys out of my pocket, get into the truck, and open the glove box. Two revolvers and a butterfly knife fall out. I dig through a few ammo clips and find a silencer. I take *Tom* from its holster and fit the two pieces together. Then I aim up.

"Oh god!" Carl screams. "Please, please- don't do this!"

The angle doesn't feel right. I could turn on the laser sight, but out of spite for The Boss, I don't. Instead I take a few steps back and say, "I'm not going to kill you. In fact, this is probably the first time in history a gun has actually been used to help someone." I fire a round in the general direction of his head. I miss, but I'm certain he feels the bullet whiz by his ear. He yelps and does what anybody does when bullets fly by their heads. He tries to drop and curl into a ball. Of course, in Carl's case he's hanging upside down. So instead of dropping, he lifts, curling his head up. Before he can lower himself, I fire a second shot at the rope above his feet. It snaps and he falls onto his back in the truck bed. The whole truck bounces a little.

Carl groans and rolls back and forth. I take it as a sign that he didn't break his spine in the landing. But I still ask if he's okay. He coughs' out, "You're crazy."

"I know you don't remember," I tell him, "But that makes us even." I go back to the glove box and toss the silencer back in. Then I feel around the floor for one of the butterfly knives and use it to cut Carl free. "Did you drive here tonight?" I ask as I help him out of the truck bed.

"Yeah," he says.

"Good," I say. "Go to a hospital. Your wrist is broken and your back is probably bruised from the fall."

I start to turn to get into the truck, but he asks, "Who are you?"

How do I even answer that question? I'm half tempted to tell the truth. It's been so long since anybody's cared to ask. I'd love to tell him that I'm Millie VanCastle, and that I didn't die in that fire a year and a half ago and I'm actually an assistant to the biggest, cruelest man alive, and that we kill monsters together. But I don't. Instead I say, "I'm Special Agent Erin Samus, FBI. I've been investigating the men who've gone missing from karaoke bars in the region. I think you were an intended victim, Carl. But you're safe now. Just get yourself to a hospital."

"Special agent?" He asks. "Are you even old enough to drink?"

"I'm twenty four," I protest, and regret it somewhat because it's true. "Anyways, thank you, citizen, and uh, have a good day."

I drive away feeling like the biggest dork alive.

I get back to the hotel and carry an armful of guns and knives into the room. Although traffic wasn't bad, helping Carl down wasted enough time. I try to hurry. I try to think of spots The Boss might reach for a weapon. Under the chair cushions. Behind the nightstand. I go into the bathroom and place a switchblade beneath the stack of towels. Walking back into the main room, I see my clothes, suitcase and book of crosswords. Removing all signs of myself, I gather them up and shove them into the closet. Then I think to put a few guns beneath the mattress. When I lift the bed, a double barrel shotgun is already lying there.

"*Daisy Duke is under the bed*," I remember The Boss calling through the bathroom door earlier in the evening. It gives me pause. Why would The Boss hide his favorite gun under the bed when he intended to chase these creatures down? Why leave it behind?

"You planned this too?" I scream. "Are you serious?" No. There's no way The Boss was capable of thinking this far ahead. The plan for weeks was that we get them someplace quiet and send them back to Hell. We watch lonely men at bars and we chase the girls down. There's no way he could've planned for this, especially since he knew- he knew I'd never go for it. Unless he got hammered and couldn't fight them until he sobered up. Back when I looked into his eyes and saw a mess of sexual fantasies, it wasn't just the moment. He was recalling encounters. He was pondering previous things he'd tried. He was- preparing. Psyching himself up.

It all comes together. This entire hunt for the three sirens was set up just so The Boss could get laid. And nothing, not I, nor their previous prey, Carl, was going to stand in his way.

I consider leaving, but as I stand there accepting The Boss as the worst human alive or dead, I see headlights stream through the curtain. I dive for the closet and shut the door.

It only takes a moment before I hear laughter outside. I hear a key scrape against the door several times before it finds its way into the lock. Then there's the sound of the door squeaking open. Through a tiny crack in the closet door, I see one of the sirens -Thelma, I think- land from being tossed onto the bed.

"Woah!" I hear Angie giggle. "Do me next!"

"Oh, I'll do all-a-y'all," The Boss says. A second later, Angie goes flying through the air and lands next to Thelma. And then Penny slowly slinks into view, stepping backwards with Gus's hand in both of hers. She guides him toward the bed and sits down with her back arched and legs spread. The Boss steps closer and she reaches for his belt buckle.

I've seen enough. I lean back, and am startled when my shoulder brushes something that isn't the wall. I barely see the gleam of gunmetal as I realize I've knocked my scattergun, and it's tipping toward the closet door.

I reach one hand out to catch it.

I use my other hand to muffle my mouth.

I feel the gun slap into my palm, but too low. The top of barrel ever so lightly taps the closet door, causing it to open another quarter of an inch.

"What was that sound?" I hear Thelma ask.

The Boss replies, "Who cares? Get naked."

I roll my eyes and lean back again, resting *Queequeg* in my lap. Outside the door I hear Thelma giggle while The Boss starts to groan. I can only imagine what Penny is doing, even if it's the last thing on Earth I'd like to imagine.

"You've put this thing to work before, haven't you?" Penny asks. "How'd you get these scars?"

"I liked what yer mouth was doin' before it started talkin'," The Boss says.

I sigh. I know how he got those scars and I'm grateful he's not about to repeat the story. I look around the closet. It's actually somewhat roomy in here. My suitcase and Gus's can both stand up. I have space to sit comfortably while avoiding the view. A scattergun can rest across my lap without touching either the suitcases or the wall. There's enough light that I spot my book of crosswords next to me on the floor with a mechanical pencil lying over it. I glance through the crack in the door again, and there's The Boss lying on his back with three naked women draped all over him. Arms, legs, and tongues are twisting in a maze of directions.

This is what my life has become, I think. I'm peeping tom to the worst porn scene ever. A hundred and fifty something year old man screws three seducing sirens of ancient times in a cheap Alabama hotel room. I try to think of a title if it was a scene from an actual movie. The best I come up with is *Snatch of the Titans*.

I sigh.

I look back down at my book of crosswords and decide that as long as everyone else enjoying themselves, I may as well indulge. I open the book to a random page and in no time I'm trying to come up with four across, a seven letter word for *cough drop*.

A few random clues later and there's a three letter word going down that starts with Z and ends with *N*. I don't have to read the clue to know that it's *Zen*.

From the room, I hear The Boss grunting while one of the sirens is screaming out, "Heee- heeee- heee!" in sharp breaths reminiscent of Lamaze. The other two are moaning to some form of prodding or another. I know there's no ignoring it, but I still try to focus on my puzzle and come up with eight across, Abraham Lincoln's birthplace. Unfortunately *Kentucky* and *log cabin* are the same amount of letters. I'll need to fill in some of the downs before I figure it out.

The evening goes on. I finish one puzzle and move onto the next. I'm trying to figure out fifteen down, a nine letter word for being highly affirmative. I'm completely stumped until Penny calls out, "Yes! Yes! Yes!"

No, I think. Then I look clues for every third word going across. Sure enough, they're all plural. I write *yesyesyes* and move on.

Not too long after, I'm stuck trying to remember the name of the drummer from Radiohead (sixteen down, sixteen letters) when I decide to peep out the closet door. Despite my hope that they're about done, The Boss is holding Angie in his arms, screwing her, while Thelma takes a moustache ride on his shoulders. Penny is lying face down on the bed with her head and a hand hanging over the edge, holding what looks like a bottle of tequila. She rolls to her side and I notice she's wearing The Boss's boots.

One of the pillows must've torn because there are white feathers floating about the room.

Another half puzzle later and I hear The Boss say, "Wait! Hang on, hang on! This ain't workin' fer me. Okay. You. Red. You twist 'round the other way- okay, now lift your arm so- yeah. Just like that. Now, Miss Penny, lean on her elbow, but cross your one leg under Thelma- no, the other leg, and higher up. Well, not quite, but it'll do. Okay, now Angie- Angie, right? Okay, well if you could arch yourself like- okay- then hang onto yonder lamp for support. Let me see, let me see- Okay, now everybody on the balls o' yer toes. Okay! Hold it!"

He continues to grunt and then approvingly remarks, "Yeah! Tha's it! Tha's it! Yeah!"

I look at my puzzle and twenty three down is a seven letter word for an unbelievable story.

Forty two across on the next puzzle asks for a five letter word for Douglas Adams's organic computer. I start to fill it in when I hear Thelma say, "Baby, aren't you ever going to come?"

Gus laughs. He says, "Shit! I did at least four times now."

"Aren't you tired?"

"Nah," The Boss shrugs. "If anything I'm just sober. But if yer worried o'er yerself, I got some extra lube here under the mattress."

I take it as my cue. I slowly stand up, *Queequeg* in both hands. My knees crick and my neck feels tight, so I peer out the crack in the door while I give myself a moment to limber up. Gus is still digging between the mattresses, probably waiting for me to jump out.

"I've got to sit down," Penny says, moving over to the chair between the dresser and bathroom. "You're something else, Gus. I am thoroughly, thoroughly going to enjoy you. She sits in the chair and crosses her legs. After a few deep breaths, she asks, "Say, what did you say these boots were made of again?"

The Boss says, "Vampire."

All three girls pause and stare at him. Penny laughs after a few seconds.

"Now, I'm sure I hid the lube under the bed," The Boss says, sounding a little annoyed, clearly at me.

"What did you say?" Penny asks.

"Oh, uh, Vampire," The Boss says. "Tracked a family o' them up north a spell back. When I was done stakin' the pussy fuckers, I figured I'd see what'd happen ta dead vampire skin in the sunlight. Turns out it don't burn. Kinda shimmers actually. Err, more like a sparkle. At least while it tans. So I said to myself, 'Well, shit! Ain't nobody e'er had a pair vampire skin boots before.'"

Normally when The Boss tells that story, people laugh and say what a great imagination he has. Or after a few awkward moments, they find an excuse to walk away. Nobody believes him. At least, nobody except those who know vampires exist. These three sirens, they all stare at The Boss with pure terror in their eyes.

"Who?" Penny starts to ask, even though I know the answer is forming in her head as the question spills from her lips. "Who are you?"

"Gus Beauregard," The Boss says. "Now, if you wouldn't mind, please take yer hot n' sexy feet out my damn boots before I spatter blood all o'er 'em."

Penny doesn't move. She just stares. I decide it's finally time to make my entrance and kick the closet door open. Stepping into the room with *Queequeg* poised at Angie's waist, I scream, "He said take his boots off! Now!"

The sirens don't move, and don't seem to panic any more than they already are. They look at me with dumbfounded eyes, and when I look into them the only image that comes back is one of Gus tearing them limb from limb. "Um? Who are you?" Penny asks.

The Boss starts laughing. "It worked!" he cackles.

To Penny I snap, "From the bar."

She shrugs. Looking at the other two girls, they both do the same. Angie shakes her head.

"I was the girl with the gun," I say.

Thelma tilts her head and squints. "Oh! Okay! It's just- I thought you were a boy when that whole gun thing happened. It's the tie-dye I think. That shirt's just not flattering on you."

Over at the bed, Gus is pounding the mattress laughing. "I can't believe you actually went for it." He pulls the shotgun from the mattress and aims it loosely at Penny, but doesn't stop laughing.

"Went for it?" Penny asks. "Please, Mister Beauregard, we didn't know it was you."

"Obviously!" I say. "He set this whole thing up to have sex with you."

"He did?"

"What?" Gus has tears rolling down his laugh lines. "Shit, that was jus' a bonus. I set all this up fer you!" He looks straight at me. "And it was jus' as funny as I knew it'd be."

"What?" I ask.

"Don' ya get it?" he says to Thelma, putting a hand on her shoulder and pointing to me. "She's a fuckin' lesbian. A dyke!"

Neither I nor the sirens say anything.

Gus continues to laugh. "She's a dyke, and I got 'er to come out the damn closet!"

"Oh, that tears it!" I scream as I un-holster *Huck* from my back. I fire a shot straight into The Boss's forehead. His laughter cuts short as he stumbles back onto the bed. His body flops onto headboard. A trickle of blood starts oozing down his face and onto his fat belly.

I holster *Huck* and aim my scattergun back at Penny. "Hang on!" She says. "Hang on! Don't shoot me!"

I keep my gun poised on her. A few white feathers float through the air between us.

"We can work this out," she says. She glances back at Gus's body, bleeding all over himself. "Who's side are you on anyway, girl?"

I cock *Queequeg*. It's chambered. I keep it aimed low, poised around their knees and hips. I'm sure it doesn't look intimidating, but its how I have to fire shotguns. I'm too light to aim straight on. When I pull the trigger, the kickback sends the gun up. If I aimed at their faces, I'd hit the ceiling. When I aim low, a pull of the trigger could result in anything from a hole in their chests to the exploding of their heads.

"Oh come now," Penny goes on. "You don't want to shoot me." She takes a step closer. "Does she, girls?"

"No," Angie says, grinning, taking a step forward.

Thelma raises her hands, pointing them at me like talons. "She really doesn't."

I aim the gun back and forth between them. "Don't come any closer," I warn them.

"Take it easy," Penny says. As she takes another step toward me, I notice the skin on her knees starts to turn to scaly. Another step and her leg looks more chicken than human. All over, her skins seems to harden. Her jawline changes and starts to protrude. Her teeth sharpen as she speaks. Her doll eyes twist closer to the sides of her face. Her pupils grow larger and larger. "You don't want to shoot us," her voice sings out in a rasp. "Look at what you just did. You saved us from Gus Beauregard! For someone with no fashion sense, you're quite a gal."

I wave the gun between the other women. Their bodies are changing too. Their fingers are snapping into claws. Instead of five toes they suddenly have three talons stretching out into points. Their hair is shrinking into their scalps and being replaced with feathers. "You don't want to come any closer," I snap.

"Come now," Penny says. "Let us say thanks and give you a makeover."

Angie adds, "You could really use it."

All down their backs, they're growing Mohawks of feathers. They extend into tails that fan out at their knees. Their shoulders crick and long webbing protrudes, starting at their armpits and growing until their wrists and hips are connected by a thick flap of skin. Feathers start growing on their arms, and the thought finally sinks in that I just watched three tramps sprout wings. And my first reaction to this is to think, "Stop calling them tramps!" But then out loud I say, "I don't wear makeup."

Thelma's knees crick as she steps toward me. "Oh, we can tell," she says.

"I'm warning you," I say. "Stay back."

Penny smirks. Or at least seems to smirk at the corners of her beak. It's hard to tell. "Well if Little Miss Rambo doesn't want our help," she says. "Maybe she can help us."

I say, "Back off."

"Ooh, feisty! You know the tough ones always taste better?" Penny asks in a now raspy voice. "What do you say, girls? A little snack before the feast?"

Thelma starts to drool out of her beak.

They keep coming closer. They just don't see it.

A thing about The Boss is, he can't be killed. At least, in the past few months since I really started losing my cool, I've never found a method that works. I've hit him with his truck. I've shoved him at a speeding train. In a few other weak moments, I've shot him, or stabbed him. It never works. Even on other hunts, nothing ever seems to kill him. I've even seen The Boss leap off a real live dragon and spatter in a puddle of its flames. He walked out charred, but somehow unscathed. No matter what anybody does, he just keeps coming. So right now, as the sirens are slowly approaching me, waiting for a hole in my defenses, that puddle of the blood on The Boss's belly has stopped dripping. Instead, it's slurping itself back into the bullet hole. Right now his skull is reforming and the scrambled eggs he calls his brains are, well, returning to whatever sludge of a mess they were before the bullet lodged in them.

"You really don't want to come any closer," I warn the sirens a final time.

Penny cackles, "Oh, why not, pretty?"

To which Gus replies, "B'cause ya'll won't see me comin'."

They turn to face him just in time to watch as The Boss swings *Daisy Duke* like a baseball bat, decapitating Thelma. It's an odd sight, and it takes a moment to process, but even her neck and head separate. Her neck splatters onto the wall. Her head drops onto the bed and bounces before rolling onto the floor. Her body collapses onto her face as Gus spins his shotgun toward Angie and pulls the trigger. She drops past the far side of the bed, out of sight, and out of this world forever.

Three seconds and two are down. Just one left.

"Sisters!" Penny snarls. "My sisters!" She jumps back and flaps her wings. The sudden gust is hard enough to knock me off my feet and for Gus to drop *Daisy Duke*. I hit the closet door and drop onto the carpet. Stunned, I feel another gust and see Penny swoop over me before crashing through the window and flying out into the parking lot.

"M'boots!" Gus screams. "Millie! Chicken Bitch is still wearin' m'boots! Catch up to us with the truck!" And at that he breaks through the door and leaps into the parking lot. I lift myself enough to see his naked, bulbous behind jiggling off into the darkness, his favorite shotgun at his side the way I've seen samurai run with their swords in the movies.

I stumble. I feel like the room is spinning. How could she do that? With just a flap of her wings? All around me, the room is in disarray. I can't tell what damage was from the wind and what was from the orgy. The bed is still in place, but everything else is in pieces. The nightstand is turned over with its lamp shattered in the corner. Two chairs and a table lay shattered around the carpet. Even the closet door has come off its hinges and is barely standing against the frame. I don't recall the room ever having a television, but it must've because there's one wedged halfway into the wall.

Outside I hear gunfire and The Boss belts out a "Woooo!"

I take a step forward and dry heave. Another and I start feeling for the keys in my pocket. How did The Boss get up so fast after that? I take a moment to crouch with my head between my knees. It's not until I realize there's a disembodied neck at my feet that I pull myself together enough to stumble out of the room.

Once in the parking lot I start breathing again. I look in every direction, but don't spot The Boss or Bird Penny anywhere. Somewhere in the distance I hear a screech, followed by another shotgun blast. "Get down 'ere, ya hellion slut!" The Boss calls out, followed by another blast. From the flash, they're already down the road. I shake myself off and get into the truck. It takes a minute to orient myself to the wheel, to the stillness of a parked vehicle, but I put the key in the ignition, throw the truck into gear and slam my foot on the gas. Then, after crashing through the hotel room wall, I put the truck in reverse, peel backwards through the parking lot, and spin around to finally join in the chase.

And here I am, driving a hundred and ten down some strange road, catching up to a naked bear of a man toting a shotgun and screaming toward the heavens to, "Get the fuck down 'ere!" As I pull alongside him he laughs, "Millie! About damn time!" He doesn't even break stride as he leaps into the truck bed and fires another shot. "Keep after 'er!"

I can't see her and I scream as much back to him.

"Jus' step on it n' stay on this road!" The Boss calls back.

I glance in the rearview mirror, and of course, I see nothing but his pecker flapping in the wind. "Boss!" I scream. "Boss!"

"Keep driving, Millie! Take the next left!"

I keep my foot on the gas. "What did she do back there, Boss?" I yell back. "She knocked me senseless!"

The Boss starts digging through some of the boxes in the truck bed and comes up with FN SCAR rifle named *Hester*. "The wind?"

"Yeah!" I see a street coming up on the left. "Hold tight!"

I'm more worried about flipping the truck than I am The Boss's safety. I clutch the emergency brake and drift as best I can, but I can feel the truck's two left wheels lifting off the ground. I look out my side window and see the tree line lowering alongside me. But then there's The Boss, one foot on the mirror and the other on the roof, keeping the weight of the truck to my side. He fires three rounds before we're moving forward again and he's thrown back from the roof. I start to brake, but through the rearview mirror I see him catch onto the truck bed and hoist himself back in. He screams for his success and fires several more rounds into sky. I don't know if he's actually aiming for anything or just enjoying himself. "Next right, Millie!" he calls down. He fires another series of shots and screams, "I fuckin' shot 'er wing up!"

At the next right, the truck starts to lift the other way. The Boss climbs onto the passenger door and opens it with one hand while firing with the other. As the truck settles from the turn, The Boss climbs into the cabin. "Keep on this road," he says before reaching under the seat for a fresh magazine. Then, returning to my question, he says, "In ancient days sirens used to sing enchanted songs to guide sailors toward their island during storms. Never thought o' it before, but it never made sense to me that them sirens would be bird women. I mean, did ya see them chicken bitches? Anyways, that there bird thing never made sense. They got the voices and the bodies to lure dumb fucks like you n' me already, right?"

I don't respond. I just keep my foot on the gas. Ahead of us, I can finally see Penny. She's struggling to stay airborne, flapping desperately above the road.

"Seems to me it makes sense enough that them sirens was creating the storms, makin' the winds to carry their voices out to sea. Otherwise, how often you think they'd really eat? The reason ya never hear o' it in the legends 's because nobody e'er saw 'em makin' the winds. Didn't need to. They was already on their island."

"Yeah?" I'm driving at top speed and she's still keeping ahead of us. All around, I can see trees and stilted houses shaking to every flap of her wings. I avoid pointing out that chickens can't fly and instead say, "What if she directs that back at us again?"

"Hm," The Boss nods. "Good point." At that he climbs back out onto the truck bed. He takes aim and fires several more rounds. Ahead of us, I see Penny spiral in the air and drop down toward the street. "Millie!" The Boss screams. "*Silvia*!"

From between the seats, I grab The Boss's bowie knife and toss it up, out the window. He catches it and calls out, "Run 'er down!"

Down the road, Penny lands on her feet and continues to run. She tries flapping her wings, but from how she arches her back I can tell she's wincing. She doesn't stand a chance.

It takes less than a second. I get close enough that just before I run her over, I slam on the brakes. The truck bows down, causing the grill to hit Penny straight on. In a plume of feathers, she's thrown forward while Gus is launched clear from the truck bed. As I skid to a stop both of them soar through the air. Penny floats limp like a rag doll. The Boss is poised with his bowie knife in both hands, firm over his head. As Penny hits the ground, The Boss brings down the blade, straight into her chest. She lands on her back. He lands with one foot on her shoulder and another on her thigh. He rides her, skidding across the ground until they come to a halt.

It's over.

I get out of the truck and slowly approach them, walking along a road rash streak of blood, skin, and feathers. To my surprise, Penny is still alive, still coughing and trying to struggle. For a second I think there's no way anybody could survive all this. The gunfire, the head on, and the knife in her chest. There's no way. But then I have to correct myself. She's not a person.

"Why?" she asks The Boss, raising a hand to clutch his wrist.

"Why?" The Boss shakes his head. "How many men you killed this century?"

"But you," she hacks. A bit of what looks like cottage cheese comes out of her ear. "We've all heard stories, but you? You're just like us. You're not one of them any more. You know these creatures, these humans are killing themselves without our help. There's no sense to it. They're fodder."

"Yeah," says The Boss. "The world's a shit covered ass hair. No questionin' that. And there ain't no redemption fer you n' me. We're damned, and we'll see ourselves n' Hell on the days we die."

"Then why?" Penny asks again. "What did my sisters die for?"

The Boss shrugs. "All right, ya got me. It's true, you n' me is jus' as rotten. But you killed a whole mess a humans. And that makes you big game. And me? I love huntin' me some big game. Fact is, I'm goin' after the biggest game in town."

"Your wife," Penny says.

The Boss nods. "You n' yer sisters? Ya'll is just trainin' fer the main event."

Penny cackles. She coughs out blood. She tries lifting herself, letting the knife cut further through her. She even pivots onto her elbows, twisting herself against the blade. "*Ante gamisou*[2]," she laughs. "You don't even know what she's planning." She jerks herself to the left and a spray of blood gushes straight up at The Boss. Penny falls limp, letting out one last giggle before a death rattle escapes her beak.

"What?" The Boss screams. "What did you say?" He slaps Penny across the face, but he's too late. She used her final breath to get under his skin, and now he's just smacking a corpse. Not that it stops him from hitting her several more times and screaming, "Wake up! What do you know about Gretchen? What? Wake up!"

Eventually he stands, wiping *Silvia* clean against his thigh. He rolls his head back and stares up into the stars. "That bitch," he utters. "That fucking, poultry cunted bitch."

"Boss?" I say. "We should probably get going."

"Yeah, Millie," The Boss nods. He looks over the dead bird woman and sighs. "Don't suppose there's reason to go back to the hotel." He starts pulling his boots from Penny's feet. They slip off easy, which isn't surprising as they're a good ten sizes too large for her, even with chicken legs. Once he's done, he takes a moment to kick her body to the side of the road. I assume as a courtesy for other drivers.

"Some of our clothes are there. A couple of guns. Nothing important."

"So if we split, you'll be stuck in that damn ugly tie-dye?" The Boss asks with a grin. "Well, that's funny. Not

---

2 I'm assuming she spoke Greek. I'm unsure of the translation.

getting you to come out the closet funny, but still. Nah, let's head back to the room. I don' feel like buyin' new luggage and it'd be cruel to leave ya with only that shirt. I'm a monster, but I ain't that terrible. Any cops are there, I'll just hypnotize 'em."

I don't even respond. I just keep watching The Boss and realize that this is how my day is ending. Even after a year and a half of following him around, I'm always left in disgusted awe at the end of a hunt. Here I am, an entire twenty four hours of being berated, shot at, and the butt of by far the dumbest joke on Earth, and now I'm watching a naked man pull vampire skin boots off the corpse of a singing chicken lady. I'm the assistant to a serial killer of the supernatural, and this is my life.

"You know something," I finally say.

"Yeah, Millie?"

Where to begin? "Um, nothing." I toss him the keys. "You drive. I feel like drinking."

Acknowledgements

This story just wouldn't have been nearly as fun if not for the patience, criticism, and support of Michael Blenman, Thomas Budday, Nathan Squires, and Yoshi Merrybird. For any of the typos missed, I guess… Oops?

Special thanks to Natalie Schunk for her beautiful watercolor art of Gus, Millie, and the three sirens.

Special thanks to Christina Irwin for creating the flattering image of me on the about the author page.

Other thanks and shout outs go to my parents, Jim and Joanne, and my three other brothers, Joshua, Daniel, and Christopher. Josh Squires, Kim Squires, Corrine Camero, Jessica Gamache, Marleija Forey, Darius Goebel, Shelly Buist, Amy Powers, Kelly Butala, Brian Sullivan, Lauren Zedan, and Anne Brege, one way or another, you all had some influence on this. Or you just make me smile. That goes a long way too, you know.

Necromantica

The Kingdom of Fortia faces an apocalypse. Orcs have invaded from the East, massacring their way straight to the holy city Dromn. While the kingdom makes its final stand, a mysterious necromancer elf and her human companion plunge through the battle in a high stakes mission to loot the king's palace. But with the city aflame and the battle stretching to every horizon, can they pull of the greatest heist ever? Can they even escape with their lives?

Whisper

In a standalone companion story to *Necromantica*, Lector Ara, a king thought to have died in a bear attack, awakens in his coffin, guided by a mysterious voice telling him that his kingdom and family are in danger.

Tender Buttons Two:
Disco Wrecklord

In 1914, American writer Gertrude Stein published the original Tender Buttons, a masterpiece in verbal cubism. Today, we live in a world of unnecessary reboots and sequels. So it shouldn't come as any surprise that we proudly present Tender Buttons Two: Disco Wrecklord, in which famed poet and muse Gertrude Stein has taken the English language hostage. It's up to the grammar police of Scotland Yard to diffuse, edit, and clarify her madness before she conjugates run on sentences improper loop loop slipping away, away, away There is no there there.

Bonnie Before The Brain Implants

Exponential Innovations: Book One

Exponential Innovations' newest employee is Bonnie Neman; one of the greatest mind's the world will ever know, a recent college graduate, and therefore qualified only for an entry level position. As an introduction to this sci-fi comedy series, Bonnie tours several labs in new her workplace, repeatedly discovering just how easy it is to reach out and touch the impossible.

About the Author

Keith Blenman hails from Metro Detroit where he teaches forensic analysis and works in a retail warehouse. He is short, chubby, and heavily tattooed.

Other books by this author

Please visit your favorite ebook retailer to discover other books by Keith Blenman:

The Vecris
Whisper: A prelude to Necromantica
Necromantica
The Girl Drank Poison
Tramp Stamp Vamp

Roadside Attraction
Book One: Siren Night
Book Two: Tramp Stamp Vamp (coming soon)
Book Three: Ruff Stuff (coming slightly less soon)

Other fiction
Bartered Breath
Bonnie Before The Brain Implants
Braaaaaains
Entrees & Statistics
Tender Buttons Two: Disco Wrecklord
Where Dogs Sweat

Non-Fiction
Character Development for Badass Writers

Deleted Scene

***

The following takes place after Millie gets dressed and before she arrives at Paulo's Karaoke Club. It was removed from the first draft for pacing and narrative purposes, but later included here for, well… other pacing and narrative purposes. Rather than include a rough preview of volume two here, I moved this scene to the end of the book as a teaser for the rest of the series.

Millie's Cab Ride

I'm told the cab will take about forty minutes to arrive, but I watch it pull into the parking lot in about five. "You got here quick!" I say, getting into the back and shutting the door. I sit straight up and my guns dig into my back. I slouch to get comfortable and I feel the barrels digging into my bottom.

"Yes, I had another fair on the island," the voice of a young girl answers from the driver's seat. "They cancelled, so here I am. You're heading up to Mobile, right? To Paulo's Karaoke Club?"

I say, "Yes," although I'm barely paying attention to her words. The sound of her has me transfixed and I lean forward to try and catch a look at her face. Although she doesn't turn around, from what I can see of her ear and jaw line, it's enough to make me ask, "I'm sorry, but how old are you?"

She covers her mouth and laugh and I'm thrown off a second time. Her giggle has a sharp rasp to it, like that of an elderly smoker. "Older than you, I'm sure," she says, in her little girl voice. Then she puts the cab into gear and hits the gas hard enough for me to brace myself between the seats. Again she cackles like an elderly woman. "Oh, forgive me," she says. "If you don't mind, I've never cared for speed limits."

She turns left and I press my hands into the seats that much harder. "Well, I…" I start to say, but she turns right and I'm pushed the other direction. I know this is insane, but for no reason I start thinking of my father and how he used to drive. Sharp turns. Breakneck speeds. I used to get rug burn in the backseat of his car from being tossed around like that, and we'd both just laugh. I should be screaming for her to let me out, but I'm strangely comfortable with her driving. "You know what? It's great. Just don't get pulled over and get me there in one piece and it's fine."

"That's the spirit!" she says. "Normally it'd be a forty minute drive, but I'll have you there in less than twenty."

"Well, don't drive too-" before I can finish the sentence, she crushes the gas pedal like she wants to hurt it and I can feel the force of our acceleration compressing me into the seat. I wince at the pistols digging into the small of my back. Originally, I'd meant to finish the sentence with *crazy* but instead I yelp, "-Christ!"

She cackles in that old woman voice. "You wish for me to slow down then?"

We zip by a speeding sixteen wheeler and around a blur vaguely reminiscent of an SUV. "You just took me off guard. That's all." I lean forward and try to get comfortable. I feel a little nauseous looking outside the cab, so instead I keep my focus on the interior. In this dark, I can't tell if the driver's hair is platinum blonde or ash white. It's only a little longer than mine, and somehow even more straggly. I notice her license displayed on the dashboard and try to read it. I squint. I adjust my glasses like an idiot. It's the darkness –not distance- that's keeping me from reading her name. I'm about to ask, but she raises her own question as soon as I open my mouth.

"So what compels you to karaoke this evening?" she asks. "Catch the singing the bug?"

"Oh, I can't sing," I tell her. "At least not in front of other people."

"Boys, then, perhaps?"

I don't know why I always get offended when people assume I'm interested in men. Really, it's a natural assumption. But it irks me just the same. Not that I say this. I don't even acknowledge sexuality with this strange, strange woman. Instead I steer clear of the subject and say, "My boss is there. I'm actually going to work."

"On a night like this your boss would force a young lady like you to work? In a karaoke bar, no less? Forgive me for prying, but are you certain his intentions are noble?"

I laugh a little. "I'm certain they're not. Actually, I doubt he'd even know that word. *Noble*. A thing about The Boss is, he's pretty much the worst man alive. Even then, calling him a man is almost an insult to all the men out there."

"Oh, come now. Surely he's not so terrible."

I consider my answer. I try looking at the driver through the rearview mirror, but it's too dark to see her face. I don't know why I'm so comfortable with her crazy driving and talking to her about The Boss. Especially with the zipping motion of everything we pass making me so nauseous. The rosary dangling from the mirror, swinging violently to her driving, isn't helping either. So instead I look down at my knobby knees. They rock a little with every bump. And I'm totally calm. "No. I don't want to oversell it, but he very well could be the source of every stereotype you've ever heard. He's crude. He's violent. He has no regard for anyone or anything. He's sexist and racist. He's drunk most hours of the day. He can't get a sentence out with inventing three new curse words. And I'm pretty sure he has sex with animals."

She rasps a little chuckle. I ignore it. I don't tell her that I wasn't joking.

"Yeah," I say. "That's exactly it. He's the embodiment of everything that *was* wrong in the world. But what's funny is, he pretty much thinks of me as everything that *is* wrong in the world today. And he doesn't even care. It's not like he's judging me for being myself. It's more like an accepted fact for him. It's his truth and he's too stubborn to get around it. 'There's Millie. She's going to Hell anyway, so I might as well take her with me.'"

A moment of silence goes by. Or at least a moment of tires flapping against pavement, squealing around bends, and ever softening honks of the various cars we pass. As the driver evens the car into a single lane she says, "But you say he does not judge you. That in men is a rare quality. And who is to say Hell is so awful?"

"Huh?" I take a second glance at the rosary hanging from her rearview mirror. The cross is inverted. Suddenly, the speed and swerving of the taxi aren't the things making me sick to my stomach. The fact that I'm so calm feels unnatural. This isn't like me. "You, um. Do you worship the devil? Is that what that is?"

He hacks a little laugh. In her innocent little prepubescent girl voice she says, "Forgive my faith," she says. "Do you wish to leave? Does my St. Peter's Cross offend? I am not a Satanist if that's what you think. Simply not one for Christ."

"Oh?" I say, hoping to sound as nonchalant as possible.

"Tell me something. When you kneel at your bedside tonight, will you pray for my soul, or just damn it?"

I don't know why, but I answer honestly. I'm fairly certain this woman is going to kill me, and I could just talk and talk and talk to her. "I used to know the difference," I tell her. "My mother and I would *daven* before bed when I was kid. Not all the time. I think she wanted me to have religion, even though she didn't have faith herself."

As I speak, I pretend to itch my back. Instead of scratching I unclasp my holsters and take the safeties off *Tom* and *Huck*. I start to wonder if there's something circulating in the air, because I'm feeling distant from my fears. All these men, I think. All these men have been disappearing from Karaoke bars. The Boss thought they were being abducted by sirens. What if they were just too drunk to drive home? What if they got into a taxi with something that shouldn't be behind the wheel? Something like her? And, the funny thing is, even with the thoughts setting in, even though I'm urging myself toward my guns, there's something so lucid in the moment. It's not like being drugged. Not quite.

"Ah! A Jewish girl then?" She laughs. Hard. "Does your boss know?"

"As if he needs one more thing to insult me with. And I'm not really anything. I was raised Jewish, but nowadays…" I trail off. "You know, he probably knows. It's not something I've hidden. He just- he wouldn't care anyway."

"Nowadays? Do you see no forces beyond those of this Earth?"

"Oh, nothing like that. I've seen enough to know there's something really negligent out there."

The driver gives a light grunt of amusement. "You know, we're not so different, you and me." she says. "I can see why Gus likes you."

I stop breathing and my heart skips a beat back into reality. She knew his name. "Gretchen!" I scream and instantly have *Tom* and *Huck* in my hands and am firing every round straight toward her. She cackles over the gunfire, continuing to swerve and steer down the street. The sharp veers of the car slap me against the door, then across the seat. My body is pounded against every surface of the cab, but I keep both guns trained on her, firing as fast as the triggers allow. I scream her name. I command her to die. I curse her with every bullet I put into the back of her head. I see red spatter across the windshield. I see holes explode foam from the seats. I see bone fragments chip from her skull. I see blood and bile spray from every hole I put in her and feel it flooding the cab up to my knees. I keep firing and feel the car spin out of control. The windows are too thick with blood for me to see outside, but I hear the screech of the tires and am blinded by flash of oncoming lights. I feel the jolt of the passenger side concaving into itself while the windows shatter. The entire cab is launched into a barrel roll above the traffic, swirling blood and shattered glass in every direction. And still, I continue to fire. Still, she continues to cackle.

Then in the flash of a bullet, it's over.

I don't know how, but I'm standing at the center of a two lane country road with both guns drawn at nothing. Only the night is in front of me. I keep one gun at twelve o'clock, and pivot the other around to six. Twelve and three. Three and nine. I point *Tom* and *Huck* in every direction, but the demon is gone. The cab is gone. There's no blood spatter. No shattered glass. Just me in the road, waving around a couple of pistols like the star of every lousy action movie I've seen in the past decade.

A purple glow catches my eye and I point both guns in its direction.

It's a karaoke bar.

I aim both guns out at my sides and then turn to face the other side of the street.

I turn back around, guns still up. There's still a karaoke bar. *Paulo's Karaoke Club*, is written in glowing, neon pink with blue microphones on either end. "Get it together, Millie," I whisper to myself. "Get it together." Whatever just happened, it's over. I still feel clean. There's no blood on me. Shattered windows haven't diced my skin in a hundred places. The weight of my guns tells me they're both fully loaded. It's like the whole drive didn't happen. I didn't just talk to The Boss's wife. I didn't just put a thousand bullets in her and her taxi. We didn't hit a car and go soaring through the air. It was just a dream. Just a bad dream, I think, and it starts to feel like one. And yet, my hands won't stop shaking. I start to lower them, but one of the neon K's flickers and I jolt both guns at it.

Millie and Gus will return in

Roadside Attraction

Part Two

Tramp Stamp Vamp

Flashing back to the beginning of the end, Millie recalls her life in the days leading up to a savage vampire attack and her first encounter with Gus.

TRAMP
STAMP
VAMP

ROADSIDE
ATTRACTION

PART TWO

A novella
by Keith

Connect with Keith Blenman

I hope you enjoyed my book. I love to connect with fans, readers, and critics alike, so please check out my social media sites. Reviews on Goodreads, Amazon, iTunes, and other retailers are also always appreciated.

Twitter: @keithblenman

Instagram: @blenmankeith

Facebook.
http://www.facebook.com/keithblenmanwriter/

Subscribe to Keith's blog:
http://keithblenman.blogspot.com

For more art by Natalie Schunk

Instagram: @Natalie.Schunk

Tumbler:
http://natalie-schunk.tumblr.com/

For more art by Christina Irwin

Instagram: @Mornia_CI

Portfolio:
http://crissyirwin1983.wixsite.com/portfolio

Get Christina's art on t-shirts:
https://flooptheferret.threadless.com/

www.ingramcontent.com/pod-product-compliance
Lightning Source LLC
Chambersburg PA
CBHW070645130626
46555CB00006B/2721

* 9 7 8 0 9 8 9 0 2 3 4 2 9 *